Hot & Wild Erotica

Just Plain Bob

Hungry
For More

WARNING

This book contains sexually explicit scenes and adult language. It may be considered offensive to some readers. This book is for sale to adults ONLY.

Please store your files wisely where they cannot be accessed by underage readers.

* * * * * * * * * * * * * * * * *

WANT FREE COPIES OF MY BOOKS?
Just visit my blog and download free copies of my books:
awesomeauthors.org/justplainbob

About the Publisher

4Fun Publishing, a member of **BLVNP Incorporated,** 340 S. Lemon #6200, Walnut CA 91789, info@blvnp.com / legal@blvnp.com

NOTE: Due to the highly emotional reaction of some people to works of erotic fiction, any email sent to the above address that contains foul language or religious references is automatically deleted by our anti-spam software and will not be seen. All other communications are welcome.

DISCLAIMER

Please don't be stupid and kill yourself. This book is a work of FICTION. Do not try any new sexual practice that you find in this book. It is fiction and not to be confused with reality. Neither the author nor the publisher or its associates assume any responsibility for any loss, injury, death or legal consequences resulting from acting on the contents in this book. Every character in this book is over 18 years of age. The author's opinions are not to be construed as the opinions of the publisher. The material in this book is for entertainment purposes ONLY. Enjoy.

I took my pad and flipped to an empty page and started writing.

OUTLINE
-Breakfast at restaurant.
-Waitress comments on fact I'm always writing.
-Tell her about erotic stories, wants to know where they come from.
-A. Personal exp.
-B. Listening to others.
-C. Out of thin air.
-STORY
- Needs a hook.
-A. She gets interested and wants to tell me about stuff that has happened to her.
- B. She gets turned on and wants to have fling and have me write about it.
-C. Need to talk to my sister/ girlfriend/cousin because she could really tell me stories.
-D. Need to get together with other waitress, she's a slut and could tell you some stories.

Need to work on it - pay more attention to what goes on in restaurant. Might get an idea.

I handed the pad back to Debbie and she read it. I saw a small smile develop and then she looked up at me. "C and D would work. My sister could tell you stuff that would curl your hair and Jen on afternoons is a perfect fit for D. My favorites are A and B, but I can't make up my mind about that. Hang on to your outline and I'll get back to you."

I tossed the outline into my briefcase with a dozen others and forgot about it.

The next day was Saturday and I never stopped for breakfast on weekends and Debbie was off on Mondays so I didn't see her again until Tuesday. I was drinking coffee and reading the Sports section of the paper when Debbie slid into the booth across from me.

"What about a combination of A and B?"

I put the paper down, "What?"

"The outline, what if you combined A and B? The idea would be to start out telling about experiences that happened and then have it lead into a fling."

Debbie was right. That would work better than either A or B standing alone. "Who do you see as the girl? Your sister, cousin or Jen from afternoons?"

"No silly, me! I'm thinking of me."

"You aren't serious?"

"Sure I am. I've had a lot of things happen to me and I think it would be a kick to tell it to someone and then to see it in print. You wouldn't use my real name, would you? And we could make up the fling part. I could tell you one of my fantasies and you could use that as the fling part and write it as if it really happened."

"I don't know, Debbie. We would have to spend an awful lot of time together for you to tell me about your past. What would your husband think?"

"He works afternoons and I have all kinds of free time in the evening. Can we do it? Please? I really want to."

What the hell, I thought, I didn't really have all that much going on in the evenings right then and a good story is a good story.

Debbie arrived at my apartment at six and I got her a beer and we sat down at the kitchen table. She was nervous and fidgety and so I asked, "Having second thoughts about this?"

"Oh no! Well, yes, kind of."

"You don't have to do this."

"But I want to. It's just that, well, I don't know. No one is ever going to know it is me, are they?"

"Not unless you tell somebody."

"You won't tell anybody? I mean, you're kind of like a doctor or a lawyer and everything I tell you is in confidence, right?"

"Not really, but think of me being like a reporter protecting his source."

"But no one will ever know, right?"

"Everyone who visits the site on the Net will know the story, but no one will know that the story is about you."

"What do I do?"

"Just tell me what you want to tell me. Start at the beginning, in the middle or just tell me about certain instances in your past - anything that might turn on someone who reads the story."

"Like what?"

"Well, most of my stuff goes to a site called Watching The Wife. The stories are about cheating wives, cheating husbands, husbands who like to watch their wives with other men, husbands who like to go down on their wives after they have been with other men and things like that. Have you ever cheated on your husband or has he ever cheated on you?"

"No one ever knows but me and you, promise?"

"Of course."

"I've cheated on Harry a couple of times."

"Does he know?"

"God I hope not."

"Then why don't you just tell me about one of those times."

"The first time was at my sister's birthday party. I'd never been unfaithful to Harry - I'd never even thought about being unfaithful - and even though I know exactly what happened and why, I still to this day, don't know how. One minute I was an innocent young wife and the next I was a cheating slut and I don't even remember the transition. Harry and I had gotten there early because I had promised my sister I would help set things up for the party. Harry and Gloria's husband Mike were in the other room and as I worked in the kitchen and dining room, I could hear snatches of conversation and laughter and it pissed me off.

"I don't know why, it was irrational, but I was pissed that Harry and Mike were having a good time while I was working to set up the party. Gloria noticed it and she told me to ignore them, "They are just men, honey, and they would only get in the way if they were out here." Still, it pissed me off and that kind of set the tone of the night for me. And then of course there is what they were talking about. I could hear most of it and most of what I heard upset me.

"They were talking about women with big tits and talking about how they would like to get this or that woman's tit in their mouth. They talked about Sylvia Meyers and that she would be at the party and wouldn't they just love to get her off into a room and play with her. When Harry mentioned that Alice, Sylvia's sister, would be at the party and wouldn't he just love to get some backseat time with her, I almost lost it, but instead I went and made myself a stiff drink.

"The guests started arriving and the party got rolling and things got worse for me. Every time I saw Harry, he was staring at Alice,

Sylvia or Mary Anson - all three have huge tits - and Harry just couldn't seem to tear his eyes away from them. A couple of times I went over to talk with him, but after a minute or so, he would walk away and a minute or two later I would see him staring at tits again. My tits aren't bad and I'm certainly not ashamed of them, but I was starting to feel inferior and that made me mad. The madder I got, the more I drank, and pretty soon I had a snootful. I wasn't passing out or falling down drunk, but I definitely wasn't thinking straight.

"I started thinking stuff like, "Okay, Harry, you don't want to pay attention to me, I'll find someone who will." I started flirting with guys; I let guys feel me up and I kept doing it where Harry could see me so it would piss him off. But every time I did it, I would glance over at him and see that he still had his eyes glued on big tits. I started swapping tongues with guys and then one guy said, "If you are going to let me play with your tits, you should at least go take off your bra so I can do it right." Tits - it was the magic word. So you want to look at tits, Harry? Well I've got somebody who wants to look at mine so fuck you.

"I went into the john and took off my bra and went back to the party. Another drink or two and I got maneuvered out of the house and into the backyard and hands were on my tits, a tongue was down my throat and the next thing I knew I was on the ground behind some bushes with a cock in my mouth and one buried in my pussy. I honestly don't remember the period from tongue in mouth, hands on tits to on the grass with two cocks in me and I have no remembrance of where the second man came from. All I know is that the two of them kept me there on the grass taking turns with me for a long, long time.

"You know what the worst part of it was for me? Actually there were two worst parts - I loved it, I shouldn't have, but I did. But the part that really pissed me off was that I lay out there on the grass for over an hour taking those two men in my mouth and pussy - over an hour - and Harry never even missed me. When I finally did get back into the party, he was still staring at Sylvia's tits.

"I knew that I should felt some remorse over cheating on him, but I didn't. On the way home, I almost told him what had happened and I actually had my mouth open to do it, but then I glanced over at him and he had a goofy little smile on his face as he watched the road and I knew that he was still daydreaming about tits so I never told him."

"How many more times did you cheat on him?"

"Three more times, not counting tonight."

"Not counting tonight?"

"Yeah. A leads to B, right? Wasn't that the plan? I tell the story, we both get horny and have a fling?"

She stood up and started to take off her clothes. I watched her and then I stood up and dropped my trousers and started to smile, "Yeah. A leads to B and you still have three more stories to tell me, right?"

"Four, sweetie. We have to count tonight too, don't we?"

Chapter 2

"How many more times did you cheat on Harry?"

Three more times, not counting tonight."

"Not counting tonight?"

"Yeah. A leads to B right? Wasn't that the plan? I tell the story, we both get horny and have a fling?"

She stood up and started to take off her clothes. I watched her and then I stood and started undressing as I smiled at her, "Yeah, A leads to B and you still have three more stories to tell me. Right?"

"Four, sweetie. We have to count tonight too, don't we?"

***

She was lying next to me stroking my limp cock and she said:

"When can we get together to do the next story?"

That's up to you. I don't have anyone to answer to, but you have a husband to worry about."

"Well, tomorrow is out, but I can make it the next day."

"That will work for me."

"If you would like, I have time for another before I have to go."

"Tell you what, sweetie, I'm willing to go as many times as you can get me up.

Debbie giggled and said, "I sure do know how to do that, lover" and she lowered her head and took me in her mouth. The woman was a blow job artist supreme! We had already made love four times in the space of two hours and that was my personal best. I had gone six times in one night, but I'm talking a full night – eight hours and a bit – but Debbie and her magic mouth had me up and running when I would have bet money that I was done for the night and now she was doing it again. It took her a lot longer, a whole lot longer, but damned if she didn't get the job done.

"You know what we haven't done yet?" she asked.

"No, what?"

"You haven't tried my ass."

"Sweetie, I'm sorry to say that I haven't tried anybody's ass."

"You've never done anal?"

"Never even came close to trying."

"Shit!"

"What's the matter?"

"I've never done it either. Harry won't do it and I hoped that as long as I was being a slut for you, you would do me there."

"I'll give it a try, but I'll tell you ahead of time that I don't know what I'm doing."

"How hard can it be? I expect that we will have to go slow since the hole is only about twenty percent as big as my pussy and it will be harder to get into. Do you have some KY or something we can use for lube?"

I didn't have any KY but I did remember that old movie, "The Last Tango in Paris" so I went out to the kitchen and got my butter dish. I spent some time greasing up her butt hole with the butter using my fingers and thumb to work it in. When she told me that she thought she was ready I buttered up my cock and put it up against her asshole.

"You sure you're ready?"

"Just go easy on me, honey. Take your time and go easy."

I pushed against the little puckered opening and my cock popped by the sphincter and Debbie gave a little cry. I stopped pushing and asked if she was all right and she said that there was a little pain, but she had expected it.

"Just go easy, honey, until I get used to it."

I went back to slowly working my cock into her anal cavity. It was tight and it seemed like it was gripping me and I suppose that the sphincter muscle was. When I was all the way in she told me to stop and let her get used to it so I stopped pushing and reached under her and used a finger to find her clit. I started rubbing it and she moaned and pushed her ass back at me.

"Okay, honey, slow and easy. Pick up the pace, but be gentle."

Half a dozen strokes and she hissed, "Oh yes, oh yes, I'm gonna like this. A little harder, honey, fuck my ass."

I had come some many times that night that it took me forever to get myself off in her ass and halfway into it she was screaming and hollering for me to fuck her harder and faster. When I finally came and pulled out of her ass, she fell forward on the bed and moaned, "Oh God, but I just have to find some way to get Harry to do this."

***

She looked up from the pages, "That is pretty much the way it happened all right. Have you proofread it yet?"

"Not yet."

"I spotted a couple of 'than' where there should have been 'that', and a 'think' that should have been a 'thing' but that's all I saw.

"Hopefully I'll catch them when I do the last spell check and then proofread it."

"I know I keep bugging you on this, but no one is ever going to know that this is me, right?"

"You just read the story, is there anything in there that identifies you?"

"No, I guess not. What do we do now?

"Well, I guess the best way would be to tell your story in sequence so why don't you tell me about your second time?"

***

It was three months later and again it was because of Harry and his obsession with big tits. It was the night of his company Christmas party. We were a little late in getting there and using hindsight I'm almost sure that he planned that way."

"Why do you say that?"

"Well, if we had gotten there early and got a table we would end up sitting with whoever came in later and saw an empty seat and came over to join us. By arriving later, Harry was able to see who was sitting where and he could join whomever he wanted. Anyway, we got there and Harry looked around at the tables and then made a beeline for one in particular and surprise, surprise, two of the women sitting there were milk cows. No, that isn't nice of me – it wasn't their fault they were blessed in the breast department or that Harry was such a damned tit freak. Mary was probably a 36C cup and Dianna was a good 38D. I looked around the room at the other tables that had empty seats and I didn't see a good set of jugs at any of them and I think that is why Harry got us to the party when he did. His goal was to sit with Mary and Dianna if he could."

"Not that there is anything wrong with what you have, but if your husband is so hung up on big tits why doesn't he just pay for you to get a boob job?"

"I offered, but he said it would be a waste of good money, money that could be best used on something else more important."

"Okay, so he seats you at a table where there are two large-breasted women, what happened next?"

"Neither Mary or Dianna was married, but Mary had brought a date. Dianna had just broken up with her boyfriend and had come to the party alone and that's where the trouble started. Harry decided that it wasn't right that Dianna not be able to dance so he appointed himself to see to it that she wasn't a wallflower. The only thing wrong with that was that he spent more time out on the dance floor with her than he did with me. The more time he spent with her, the more pissed off I got. Add to that the fact that the drinks were flowing and alcohol always tends to lower my inhibitions a little and I finally reached a point where I said, "Fuck you, Harry!" I started looking around the table and checking out the guys.

It was a large table and besides Harry and me, there were three couples, two single guys and Dianna. That was another thing that pissed me off. With two single guys at the table, why the hell did Harry think he had to be the one to keep Dianna from sitting out the dances? I downed another drink and when the band came back, I started flirting with the two single guys and the next time Harry went out on the dance floor with Dianna, one of them, Tom was his name, asked me to dance. I stayed out on the floor with him for the last two songs of the set and while we danced, we talked. Actually he did most of the talking and I just listened. He complimented me on my dress, told me he liked the way my hair framed my face and as he talked he pulled me closer and closer to him and I felt his erection pushing into my leg. He told me that Harry was a fool for ignoring me and spending his time on Dianna. He had just finished telling me that if he had a woman like me, he damned sure wouldn't ignore her when the band announced they were taking a break. I thanked Tom for the thought and he walked me back to the table.

I downed another drink and when the band came back, Ben, the other single guy, asked me to dance. Either he or Tom kept me out on the dance floor for the band's entire eight song set and Harry never even missed me.

I wasn't stupid. I knew that Tom and Ben were trying to hustle me. They didn't expect to get anywhere that night, but they both worked hard at trying to get me to give them my phone number and to agree to meet if only for coffee. I had no intention of doing either, giving them my number or meeting them, but while I didn't say yes, I didn't say no. I wanted to keep them interested. I had the silly idea that Harry would see them sniffing after me and he would get his head out of his ass and protect his territory. Silly me right? Protect his territory when there were big tits to ogle and lust after? Not my Harry!

It was about two and a half hours into the party and I'd had enough alcohol by then to lower my inhibitions, and that combined with my being pissed at Harry led me to do a few things that I would not normally do. When either Tom or Ben pushed their erections into my leg or lower belly, I pushed back. When a hand slipped down my back and ended up resting on my ass, I didn't protest or push it away. When Ben put one of his hands on my right breast all I did was say, "Naughty, naughty" and push it away when what I would normally have done was slap his face and walk away leaving him on the dance floor.

What I was trying to do was get Harry's attention, but all I was accomplishing was making myself horny. Talk about a situation that sucked. I was horny as a goat on the one hand and on the other, I was so pissed off at Harry that I was going to cut him off for a week.

I was on the dance floor with Mary's date and she was dancing with Tom. Harry was – where else – on the dance floor with Dianna. They – 'they' being whoever it was who decorated the room for the party – had hung a large clump of mistletoe from the ceiling and they had rigged a baby spotlight to shine on the space just under it. I just happened to be looking that way when Dianna and Harry moved into the spot lit area and stopped. Harry kissed Dianna and it wasn't just a peck either. Even from halfway across the room, I could tell that there was some tongue involved. My first impulse was to storm over to them, push them apart, punch Harry in the face and pull Dianna's hair out by the roots. That's what I wanted to do, but I guess that basically, I'm a coward so what I did was tell Mary's date that I suddenly felt light-headed and I asked him to take me back to the table.

I was sitting there staring down into my drink when Tom said, "You seem upset" and I told him that I was. He asked if there was anything he could do and I told him he could tell me where to find a pay phone so I could call a cab to take me home. He asked "What about Harry?" and I said, "Fuck the son of a bitch." Tom said I wouldn't need to call a cab, that he was getting ready to leave anyway so he would be glad to give me a lift.

"You sure it wouldn't be any trouble?" I asked.

"Not a bit."

"I need to hit the ladies room first and then I'm ready to go."

When I got back from the bathroom, I told Tom I was ready.

"You going to tell Harry you're leaving?"

"No. The shit head has ignored me all night, he won't even know I'm gone. Let him waste an hour looking for me when he is ready to leave."

"Okay, let's go."

It was dark in the parking lot and it wasn't until the interior light in Tom's car came on that I saw Ben sitting on the back seat. I looked at him and then at Tom and Tom shrugged his shoulders and said, "Ben was leaving too so I offered him a ride."

Like I was too stupid to know what they were hoping for, right? I could read their minds. "She's pissed at Harry, she's had a lot to drink, she's been pushing back when I poked my cock into her so if I play it right I might get a piece of her sweet ass."

I got in the car and gave him directions and then I sat there staring out the passenger side window and looking at the houses, yards, trees and parked automobiles that we passed. I was fuming inside over Harry and the way he lost all common sense when he got close to a big pair of boobs. And I of course remembered the last party we were at and what had happened to me there. I was already horny as hell and the memory of that time when those two men had me on my knees and on my back out in that backyard just made it worse. Being in a car with two guys who wanted to make my horniness disappear didn't help matters any.

I was still looking out the side window when Tom said, "We have to go right by my place to get to yours. Would you like to stop for a drink?"

A lot of things went through my mind just then. I wondered if he thought I was dumb, or just an easy piece of ass, or maybe he thought I just might like some company just then. I knew what he was hoping for and that, in fact, he and Ben were both hoping for the same thing. I was pissed at Harry and thinking about how to get back at him and remembering the time at the last party and how much I had loved it when the two men got me going.

I turned away from the window and looked over at Tom for several seconds and then I said, "No, if we go to your place I'd get too comfortable and lose track of time and that wouldn't be good because I need to be home when Harry gets there. Find us a dark place to park." I swear his jaw dropped. I had actually caught him by surprise, but he was even more surprised when I climbed over the seat and got in back with Ben.

I'll show Harry I thought to myself, he isn't going to get as much fun from looking at Dianna's tits as I'm going to get from putting out for Tom and Ben. I had Ben's cock out of his trousers and in my mouth and was well on the way to getting him off when Tom finally found a place to park. I was on my knees deep throating Ben when Tom moved in behind me. He didn't even try to pull my panties down; he just pushed the crotch gusset to one side and poked his cock at my hole. I'd been horny most of the night so I was wet enough and three strokes had him all the way in. Tom grabbed hold of my hips and started fucking me. Tom was a talker and as he fucked me he kept up a running line of chatter:

"Damn but you are tight, girl. Doesn't Harry ever use this pussy? Is that why you are so easy, you need more cock than you can get at home? I'm going to give you all you can handle, baby; I'm going to fuck you so good that you will be begging me for more."

Well, the fact of the matter was that he was fucking me good and I decided to see if I couldn't wind him up a little. I took my mouth off Ben's cock and moaned:

"Oh yes, honey, fuck me good. Make me your slut, honey, come in me, knock me up, give me a baby. I'm at my most fertile honey, cum in me, make me pregnant."

It was all bullshit of course. Two years earlier I'd had a hysterectomy and pregnancy was no longer a worry for me, but Tom and

Ben didn't know that and the more I egged him on, the harder he fucked me and the harder he fucked me, the closer I came to having an orgasm.

Ben kept trying to get my mouth back on his cock and I finally told him no. I told him that if I kept sucking him off he would cum and then when Tom came all I'd have was two limp dicks.

"Keep your hard on" I told him, "So you can fuck me when Tom finishes."

Just about then Tom moaned, "Here it comes, I'm gonna fill you, here it comes" and I felt him shoot into me. Ben was struggling to get up so he could take Tom's place in my pussy – there isn't a whole lot of room in a back seat when three people are there having sex - and Tom was pulling out of me and asking if I was going to name the baby after him. Ben laughed and said:

"What makes you think it's going to be yours? Maybe my sperm is stronger than yours and I might be the daddy."

By then I was off my knees and lying on my back and Ben was pulling off my panties. Tom moved to where he could get his dick in my mouth and I started licking our combined juices off of it and then I went to work at getting him hard again. Ben pushed my legs apart and I had one draped over the back of the front seat and the other was sticking almost straight up and I had the foot planted against the roof of the car. I noticed that the thin four-inch heel had poked a hole in the head liner and I wondered if Tom would ever notice and if he did would he know how it happened.

Ben drove into me so hard he took my breath away and then he started fucking me hard. I was moaning and gurgling around Tom's cock as Ben started building my fires again. Ben was a silent fuck so the only noises in the car were my continuing moans and Tom's constant babble. The man just could not keep his mouth shut.

"That's it, honey, suck it, suck it good. Get it hard for me, baby, iron-bar hard. I don't want you to ever forget it, baby, I want you to remember my cock forever. Get it hard, sweetie, I want another chance at knocking you up."

Ben was doing a fine job of fucking me and I took my mouth off of Tom long enough to give him some encouragement:

"Fuck me hard, Benny" I said to him, "Make me cum, sweetie, give me a baby, help me get even with Harry, give me a baby, sweetie, knock me up and give Harry a kid to raise."

Tom pulled my head back to his cock and for the next couple of minutes, I just lay there and moaned while the two men used their cocks on me. Ben brought me to one orgasm and I was well on my way to another when he groaned, "Shit! I'm going to lose it, I don't want to lose it, I want to stay hard and fuck you forever. Oh fuck, I'm losing it."

I pulled my mouth off Tom and cried, "No, not yet, please not yet, just a little bit more, please, baby, please, I'm almost there" but the words weren't even all the way out of my mouth when I felt him splash my insides. "Get off, get off of me" I cried, "Get out of the way so Tom can get on me and get me off. Hurry damn it, hurry."

Ben jerked himself out of me and tried to get out of the way while Tom scrambled to get from my head to my pussy. Did I mention how cramped a back seat can be when there are three people having sex on it? Anyone outside looking in would have laughed their asses off at that Chinese fire drill. The boys finally got relocated, but by then I'd lost the edge.

No need to get repetitious here so I'll just say that Tom fucked me while I sucked on Ben, Tom and I both came and then Tom got in the front and pointed the car toward my house and Ben fucked me on the back seat as we drove.

I did get a big buzz over something that happened on the way home. We got stopped by a red light and while waiting for the light to change, Tom was watching Ben fuck me in back when a car full of teenaged boys pulled up next to us. I was lying on my back and I couldn't see them, but I could hear them calling out and asking if they could be next. Tom laughed and said:

"How about it, sweetie? Want me to pull over so the four of them can get a taste?"

"You will never know how much I wanted to do it, but of course I couldn't. 'Get me home, Tom,' I said, "I have to beat Harry home.'"

"What if he is already there?"

"He won't be. He's never in his life left a party until he was one of the last ones there."

Ben was just getting me off when Tom pulled into my driveway and after I came, it was another three minutes before he got his rocks off. Tom kept looking over his shoulder nervously while Ben and I finished up. I guess he was scared that Harry might pull in behind us.

As I was getting out of the car, both guys were still trying to get my phone number and to commit to another meeting. There wasn't a chance in hell that I would see them again, but I wanted them to keep their mouths shut so I told them that as long as Harry never found out what we had done, I'd think about it and get back to them. I kissed them both goodnight and went into the house. I showered and douched and then went to bed.

I was sound asleep when Harry got home so I don't know what time it was. I won't go into all the bullshit that took place the next morning other than to say that it was two weeks before Harry got a piece of my pussy again.

***

"So, that's my story of the second time I cheated on Harry. Are you ready?" she asked me as she started to unbutton her blouse.

"Am I ready?"

"Yeah. A leads to B remember?"

"Oh yeah, right, A leads to B" I said as I stood up and pulled down my zipper.

Chapter 3

I was sitting in a booth at the restaurant when Debbie came over to refill my coffee cup. She topped me off and then sat down and asked me:

"How's the second story coming along?"

"I finished it last night and I also posted the first one on one of the sites I use. It should be up for viewing by tonight."

"You have any plans for tonight?"

"No, why?"

"Harry is spending the weekend at his folk's place. He's going to help his dad replace the roof on the barn. I couldn't go because I have to work tomorrow. I could come by and tell you about my third time cheating on Harry and maybe read the story you posted."

"You read it the last time you were over."

"I know, but I'd kind of like seeing it the way everybody else is going to see it."

"Make it around six and plan on having dinner. I'm going to make meat loaf."

"Oh wow, good in bed and you cook too. I just may have to dump Harry and chase after you."

"I'd at least wait until after you taste the meatloaf before you make that decision."

She laughed and got up and went back to work.

***

Debbie arrived at ten to six and when I opened the door and let her in, she handed me a paper bag.

"You made the dinner so I'm supplying the wine and the dessert."

"Dessert?" I asked as I looked in the bag and found two bottles of Merlot. "What dessert?"

"Me, silly."

We ate dinner and polished off one bottle of the wine. I opened the other, refilled our glasses and then we went into the living room and got comfortable, Debbie on the sofa and me in the easy chair. I picked up a pad of paper and a pen from the end table and waited for Debbie to begin.

"You are going to think I'm awful, but it wasn't Harry and his fixation on big tits that led to my third infidelity, it was the first two that were responsible."

"How is that?"

"After the episode in Tom's car, I went home determined that I would be a good girl from then on. The first time was over some teasing that got out of control and it happened. The second time it happened because I was in a jealous snit over what Harry was doing with Dianne. When Tom dropped me off I rushed into the house, showered and douched real good before going to bed and then I lay there looking up at the ceiling and wondering what the hell my problem was. So Harry liked looking at tits, so what? Was he fucking the big-titted bitches? I didn't really think so. As far as I knew Harry looked at them and got himself all fired up and then came home to me to put out the flames. Harry was a good husband and he deserved better than what I was doing to him. I fell asleep promising myself I'd never get upset with Harry over his thing for big tits ever again. And I haven't.

I didn't realize it that night as I fell asleep, but those two affairs that I'd had changed me. It was three days later, when I came back to work after being off five days, that I began to become aware of the change. The very first customers that day were two guys who worked for the city and as I poured their coffee, I wondered what the two of them would be like if I had them in bed with me. I never had had those kinds of thoughts before, not even about single guys, but from that day forward, two guys at a table or in a booth got me to wondering what it would be like for the three of us. I suddenly realized that I had a hunger for sex with multiple partners. I wanted a cock in my mouth and in my pussy at the same time. I wanted the limp cock leaving my pussy to be immediately replaced with another hard one. I had the hunger, but I had promised myself that I was going to be a good girl and by God I was going to be one.

It went on like that for months. Two guys sitting together would get me to wondering. You know me, I flirt. I flirt a lot. It doesn't mean anything, it is just something I do to try and increase the size of the tips I get. A lot of guys flirt back. They don't expect it to turn into anything; it is just fun and joking around.

Well, there are two guys who come into the restaurant three and four times a week, you would know them if you saw them, and I would flirt with them and they flirted back It went on for several months and one day one of them said:

"Debbie, love, when are you going to stop fighting it and break down and give us a taste?"

To this day I have no idea why I did what I did because I had promised to be good, but I had loved being used by two men at once and Harry was working swings that month so I knew I'd have the time. I just smiled down at the two of them and said:

"I usually stop at Tony's for a drink when I get off work at three."

After I'd walked away from the table, I asked myself just why in the hell I'd done that and by two-thirty, I'd made up my mind to go straight home and stay the hell away from Tony's Bar and Grill.

By three-twenty, I'd finished my vodka tonic and had decided that they thought I was just kidding them and I was getting ready to get out of the booth and leave when they came in the door. Only there weren't two of them, there were three. I sat there watching them walk toward me and I was torn between wanting to stay and wanting to get up and run. My pussy had been tingling all afternoon at the thought of two hard cocks working me over, but three? I didn't know about that. Then I told myself I was getting anxious over nothing. They wouldn't have invited a third guy without checking it out ahead of time with me. The third guy was probably just going to have a drink with us and then leave.

By the time I had run all of that through my head, it was too late to run. They were at the booth and Ralph slid in next to me so I was between him and the wall. Todd and the third guy, he was introduced as Dave, sat across from Ralph and me. Four drinks later Ralph said:

"If you don't mind, Dave would like to join us."

By that time I wouldn't have minded if every man in the bar would have joined us. For as long as he had been sitting there Ralph had had his hand up my skirt and had been fingering my pussy. Todd had reached under the table and had taken hold of my right ankle and had lifted my foot up to his crotch. He took my shoe and sock off and he had his cock out and was stroking it with my foot. I was so hot and wet I thought I could hear my wet pussy dripping on the floor. When Ralph asked me about Dave I said that I didn't care, but that I was more than ready to get out of there.

Todd and Ralph walked me out to Ralph's car and Ralph told me to ride with them and they would bring me back later for my car. I was no sooner on the front seat between the two of them when Todd had the fingers of one hand up my leg and in my pussy. He used his other hand to unzip himself and take out his cock. I knew what he wanted and so I reached over and grasped his cock and started stroking it.

On the other side of me, Ralph was watching out of the corner of his eye while he drove and so he took out his cock. So there I was, sitting between two men with a cock in each hand and I was slowly jacking them off in broad daylight as we drove down Main Street. I just knew that everyone in town could see me and what I was doing, but I didn't care, all I wanted to do was get to a flat surface and fuck.

We pulled into the apartment complex on Union Street and they hustled me out of the car and into an apartment on the first floor. The door wasn't even fully closed behind me and they were taking my clothes off. As soon as I was naked, Ralph pushed me to my knees in front of him and I started sucking his cock while Todd undressed. Once he was naked, I moved over and sucked his dick while Ralph stripped and then they picked me up and carried me into the bedroom. They set me down on a king-sized bed and then they both climbed on it with me.

My body was tingling and I was rubbing my clit in anticipation. I was going nuts waiting for a hard cock to slide into me. Ralph moved over me and I spread my legs as wide as I could and he placed his cock against my love hole and then asked me if I was ready and I hissed out a yes. He shoved hard and in one stroke buried himself deep in my hot wet pussy. Todd moved up to my head and offered his cock to my mouth and I took it.

You're a man so I can't expect you to understand how I felt at that moment. I was penetrated by two men and I was loving it. The feeling is indescribable. We soon had a rhythm going. Ralph would push into my pussy and that would push my mouth up at Todd's cock and as Ralph pulled back for the next in stroke, I would push my ass back to follow him and that would move my mouth backwards on Todd's cock.

Todd was pretty close to cumming when there was a knock on the door and Todd pulled out of my mouth and went to let Dave in.

Ralph was pounding away at me and I felt that stirring in my center that told me I was getting ready to orgasm.

"Hard, baby, hard" I cried to Ralph, "I'm almost there, baby, get me off, make me cum and he rammed me hard a couple of times and I exploded. Ralph kept pumping and maybe thirty seconds later, he pushed his load into me. I wasn't even down from my high when Ralph got out of the way and let Todd mount me. Todd had been close to cumming when he got up to let Dave in, so he didn't last very long. He fucked me hard for maybe two minutes and gave me one small orgasm before he spilled himself into me.

Todd was no sooner out of the way than Dave was on me and thrusting deep. My body was on fire. I was lying there with my eyes closed and luxuriating in the feeling when a cock poked me in the cheek. I opened my eyes and saw Ralph looking down at me and smiling as he offered me his limp cock.

"Make it live" he said, "Bring it back to life so it can worship that hot body of yours some more."

I opened my mouth and took him in and after that it all became a blur as the three of them used me for their pleasure while giving me all the sex I could handle. The best part for me that night was when they all three wanted to do me at the same time. Todd called it 'making me air tight.' He got on his back and had me sit down on his cock and then he hugged me to his chest while Ralph pushed his cock into my ass and then the two of them started fucking me and Dave stepped up and I sucked his cock. It was just fucking wild.

I realized what it was that made multiple partners so appealing to me. There was always a hard cock ready to take the place of one that had just gone limp. I came so many times that I was almost too weak to stand up to get dressed.

I didn't want it to stop. I wanted to stay in that apartment and be their fuck toy until none of the three could get it up again, but I had to get home before Harry so I could shower and douche and be ready for him in case he wanted to make love when he got home. No, that wasn't true. The way I felt right then, Harry was going to get laid if he wanted it or not. I'd rape him if I had to.

After I was dressed, Ralph drove me back to the bar so I could pick up my car and on the way, he asked me if when we could do it again and I told him I'd have to think about it and let him know. He dropped me off, I picked up my car and drove home.

"Did you have to rape Harry that night?"

"No, as soon as I put my hand on his cock, he was up and ready."

"Did you ever do it with Ralph, Todd and Dave again?"

"One more time with Ralph and some others, but I never did it with Dave or Todd again."

"Ralph and some others?"

"Yeah, sweetie, and that's the next story. Ready for the A leads to B part?"

I smiled as I stood up and started to take my trousers off. She smiled back and said, "I hope you took your vitamins today. Harry isn't home tonight and I don't have to hurry to beat him home. How do you feel about waking up in the morning with a slut?"

Chapter 4

I was busy pounding away on my computer keyboard when the doorbell rang. I got up to answer it and found Debbie standing there.

"I know you weren't expecting me, but Harry got a call and had to leave. Can I come in?"

I told her that of course she could and I stepped aside and then closed the door behind her. "What's going on?" I asked.

"You know the barn that Harry helped his dad put a new roof on? Well, Harry's dad went back up on it to put up a weather vane or lightening rod or something and he fell off. He broke a leg and Harry has to go down there for a few days to take care of the animals until his mom can hire someone. I thought I'd take advantage of the situation and come over here and tell you the last story of my cheating on Harry."

And then she chuckled and said, "Well almost the last, there's still you. Got time to listen to me talk?"

I had her sit on the couch and went out into the kitchen, poured two glasses of wine and then went back into the living room. She took a sip of the wine and then said:

"I really was a whore for the last one."

"How so?"

"I let myself be gangbanged by five guys."

"Tell me about it."

***

"After my time with Ralph, Todd and Dave, I promised myself that I was going to be good from then on. Do you have any idea of how hard it is to be good? Especially when you are constantly reminded of how good it was being bad? That's the position that I found myself in. Every day, Ralph and Todd would come in for breakfast and every time I saw them, my pussy would get wet as I remembered what we had done.

It was a week before Ralph asked me when we could get together again and that was my opportunity to tell him sorry, that I'd loved it, but it was a one-time thing that I'd never do again. But I didn't say that. I just said that I didn't know. From then on, once or twice a week, Ralph would ask me if I was ready yet and I would always answer no and then say something like, "I can't this week because…" and then I'd give some lame excuse instead of just saying that I was never going to do it again.

The more he asked the more I remembered how much I had loved it and a couple of times the memory turned me on so much that I had to go to the bathroom and get myself off. That went on for almost two months, months during which all I thought about was how good it felt to have three men using me, bringing me to orgasm after orgasm after orgasm.

And then one day Ralph was in the restaurant by himself and as I was refilling his coffee cup he said:

"You ready yet, sweetie? You want to, it is written all over your face every time I come in here."

He was right, I did want to and I was more than ready, but I was all set to give some excuse when he said:

"Dave and Todd won't be there, but I can have a few others there to show you a good time."

I don't know why I said it, to this day I really don't know, but I said:

"How many is a few?"

Ralph smiled at me and said, "A few is as many as you want it to be. Do you have a favorite number?"

I did. My lucky number has always been five and without even realizing what I was doing, I said, "Five. My favorite number is five."

"Consider it done, sweetie. Tony's at three, right?"

I nodded a yes and went back to work. Ten minutes later, I was calling myself all kinds of stupid. I couldn't believe that I had agreed to do it. Well I wasn't! No way was I going to do it. No way I was going to stop at Tony's after work, but for the rest of the morning, all I thought about was the number five. By noon I was so hot that I had to go into the bathroom and finger myself off. Five cocks. Five hard cocks, one for each hole and two left over – one for each hand. Just the thought had me climbing walls and Harry was gone to his folk's place for three or four days.

***

At quitting time, I got in my car and pointed it in the other direction from Tony's. I actually got almost five miles before I hung a U-turn. Ralph was sitting in a booth waiting for me when I walked into the bar.

"You want a drink or three first, or do you want to get right to it?"

I hesitated for a second or two – my last chance to run – and then I said, "Let's get to it before I chicken out."

"Atta girl" he said as he slid out of the booth and led me out to his car. We got in and he unzipped his jeans and took out his cock and looked over at me. I knew what he wanted and I moved over and lowered my head and started to suck him off as he started the car and pulled out of Tony's parking lot.

You have no idea how erotic it can be giving a man a blow job in broad daylight as he drives down Main Street. No one from the sidewalk could see me lying there with my head in Ralph's lap, but twice a pick up truck that was high enough for the driver to see down into the car drove next to us and watched for several blocks. One even honked his horn and gave Ralph a 'thumbs up'. I kept my face buried in Ralph's lap so the two drivers never saw my face, but knowing that they had seen me doing what I was doing was a massive turn on for me.

We pulled into the parking lot of Ralph's apartment and he parked and sat there until I got him off. I swallowed every drop I could coax out of him and after I had licked his cock clean and tucked him back in his pants I sat up and Ralph said:

"Okay, sweetie, let's get this party started."

We got out of the car and walked to his apartment and he opened the door to let me in. I saw four guys standing there waiting and I didn't know any of them. I almost turned and ran – almost. As the apartment door closed behind me, Ralph put a hand on my shoulder and pushed downward and I knew what he wanted me to do. I sank to my knees as Ralph said:

"Okay, sweetie, I've bragged on what a great little cock-sucker you are so how about showing these boys that I wasn't lying to them."

A man moved in front of me and my eyes were level with the bulge in his trousers. I reached up and undid his belt buckle and then pulled his zipper down and then I pulled his pants and under shorts down to his ankles. His cock leapt out at me and I took it in my hands and just held it for a moment and felt his heat. I looked around the room and shivered in anticipation of all those cocks filling me.

The cock in my hands had a drop of pre-cum in its pee hole and I leaned forward and licked it up and then I took him in my mouth. I felt his hands on my head pulling me forward onto his meat and it slid over my tongue until it touched the back of my throat and then he started fucking my face. I had one hand on his balls, massaging them and after a couple of minutes, I felt them tighten and his cock started throbbing and his cum shot out, hit the back of my throat and slid down into my belly.

God, I couldn't believe the slut I had become. On my knees in front of a man I had never seen before, and taking his juice down my throat. I pulled back and his cock fell from my mouth and another man stepped up to take his place. I could see the pre-cum leaking from the head of his cock and I licked it up and then it was one cock after another until I had sucked all of them off.

They lifted me from the floor, stripped me and put me on the bed. Hands were on my breasts squeezing them and tweaking the nipples, fingers were in my pussy and a finger was teasing my ass. My legs were pulled apart and a cock drove into me. Another one pushed at my lips and I opened my mouth. Hands grabbed my head and held it while the man fucked my face. The cock in my pussy was driving hard and I came so hard I saw stars. The cock in my pussy splashed my insides and then pulled out and another cock drove in to me. The cock in my mouth spurted and was pulled out only to be replaced with another. I was having orgasm after orgasm as my tits were sucked and my mouth and pussy fucked.

Suddenly all the cocks were pulled away from me and I cried out, "No, no, not yet" and someone laughed and hands pulled me up. I was lifted and then lowered down on a hard cock and I moaned out, "Oh yes, oh yes, oh god yes" as it sliced up into me and then my moans were choked off by a cock being shoved into my mouth.

I felt fingers probing my ass and then a hot, stabbing pain as a cock pushed into my butt. The pain slowly disappeared and was replaced by pleasure. The cock in my pussy and the cock in my ass settled into a rhythm and another orgasm swept over me and I lost it. I totally lost it. For the next three hours, it was like one continuous orgasm and I was just a mindless fuck toy as cock after cock emptied in my pussy, my ass and my mouth.

And then it was over. They were getting dressed and I was lying on the bed a fucked-out mess. I was covered in cum from the top of my head to the soles of my feet. My pussy and ass were stretched, my jaw was sore and cum was running out of me like water from a tap.

And I had loved every fucking second of it.

Ralph had to carry me out to his car because I had trouble walking. It was a damned good thing that Harry was going to be gone for several days because it would be at least two or three before I could let him near either of my holes. When I got home, I soaked in the tub for two hours before I went to bed and slept like a baby.

***

"Did you ever see Ralph again?"

"Other than in the restaurant? No. I've wanted to, God knows I've wanted to, but I haven't."

"Why not?"

"Because, believe it or not, I love Harry and I could see that if I kept up with what I was doing, it would catch up with me sooner or later. And I could see where I was heading. I had loved it when Tom and Ben used me in the car on the way home from the Christmas party. I went crazy with Ralph, Todd and Dave and the gangbang with the five guys was intense and even as Ralph was driving me back to my car, I was wondering what six, seven or even ten men would be like.

After soaking in the tub that night, I had gotten into bed and had lain there staring up at the ceiling and thinking about what I had done, what I wanted to do and what could happen if I did it. It was clear to me that if I planned on staying with Harry, I had to stop. I had to go cold turkey and I didn't do bad at it."

"What does that mean?"

"It has been almost three years now since the gangbang and I've been a good girl. Well at least I was a good girl until you came along."

"Why did you fall off the wagon with me?"

"Short answer to a long story? I found out something about myself with my infidelities. I'm a slut and one man isn't enough for me. I've fought it for three years now, but the bottom line is that even though I love Harry to death, by himself he isn't enough for me."

"So why me?"

"Opportunity, sweetie. I've been thinking of getting Harry some help for a while now. I needed someone I considered safe, someone I could trust to keep quiet about what we were doing and when I found out about your little hobby I picked you."

"So you are expecting that we will have a continuing relationship?"

"That's what I want, sweetie, but of course it will be up to you. Think about it, but while you do A leads to B right? Let's get to the bedroom, sweetie."

The End

Here is a sample from another story you may enjoy:

JUST PLAIN
BOB

"Hot Erotica"

NAUGHTY
&
NICE

FROM LOVING WIFE TO SHARED WIFE

It was going to be as bad as she feared. Jake met them when they arrived and when he took her hand she suddenly felt weak in the knees. He leaned forward and kissed her on the cheek and she felt her pussy tingle and it was all she could do to suppress a moan.

"It has been too long since I saw you last. You look lovely tonight." Turning to Gary he said, "Best you keep a close eye on her tonight. The way she looks, someone is sure to want to steal away with her. Come on, let me show you two to the bar."

Jake left them at the bar where they gave their orders to the bartender hired for the party. As Jake walked away Gary said,

"I think he likes you. In fact, seeing the way he checked you out when we walked in the door I wouldn't doubt that he was thinking the same thing I was thinking when I asked you for a quickie." He laughed, "How about it, babe, want to make me a vice president?"

She punched his arm. "You are a pervert, but then again maybe I might like being the wife of a vice president. What do you think it would take? A blow job? A quickie on the patio? Maybe meet him in a motel room and give him an afternoon of bliss? You want to watch?"

Gary laughed, took her by the arm and then they circulated and socialized. Twice she needed to go to the bathroom and both times she forced herself to wait until another woman had to go and then she tagged along. No way was she going to give Jake a chance to catch her alone the way he had the first time.

She managed to be talking with someone every time he came up to her and she had refused to let him separate her from who she was socializing with. But as determined as she was to avoid him, he was just as determined to get her alone and he finally managed it and he did it in a way that scared her. It scared her because she discovered that her secret wasn't all that much of a secret to some people.

Irene Jacobs, the wife of the vice president of finance, came over to her and started talking. After several minutes Irene said she wanted a breath of fresh air and asked her to come along out to the patio. Irene led her out to a dark corner behind the gazebo where she saw Jake waiting. Irene went to him and kissed him while running a hand over the bulge in Jake's trousers. She broke he kiss and said:

"Here she is, baby. Save a little for me, okay?" and she walked away.

Jake walked over to her and pushed her back against the wall of the gazebo and held her there with one hand while he used the other to unzip himself and take out his cock. He let go of her and said, "You know what to do." She did know and she slowly slid down the wall of the gazebo until her face was level with Jake's manhood. She looked up at him and saw him looking down at her with a smirk on his face.

"Do it!" he growled and she leaned forward and took his cock in her mouth and started giving him a blow job. Jake chuckled and said, "You look good with a dick in your mouth. That's it, baby, suck it, get me rock hard. I want it to feel like an iron bar when I shove it in your tight asshole."

She almost came when he told her he was going to take her ass and she increased her efforts to get him as stiff as she could. After several minutes he stepped back and his dick fell from her mouth.

"Stand up and take off your panties."

She did what she was told and then Jake told her to turn around, lean against the gazebo and spread her legs. She did and he moved behind her. She felt his cock head against her anal orifice and she moaned and shoved herself back at him.

"That's it, my slut," Jake said. "Take it in your ass, baby. Push back, you do the work."

She moaned and shoved back at him and felt the head of his dick pop past her sphincter. He laughed and said:

"Good little slut. Take it, baby, take it all."

She cried out, "Oh God" and slammed her ass back at Jake and felt his length slide in. He gripped her hips and began to fuck her hard. "Yessss," she hissed as he drove into her. "Yessss, so good, so good, take my ass take my ass."

"You like my dick in your ass?"

"I love your dick in my ass. I love you humping my ass."

"Are you my slut?"

"Oh God, oh yes, oh yes, my ass."

"I asked you if you were my slut."

If you enjoyed this sample then look for **Naughty And Nice**.

Also by this Author:

The Prodigal Family: The Abbotts

Watching My Shared Wife

The Waitress and the Runaway Husband

Baiting Mr. Little

Too Hot for Henry

Chuck's Fantasy

The Redhead's Desires

Rescued at Riley's

His Every Fantasy

Open Mike Night

Pursuit for Revenge

Why Does He Do That?

Halloween & Drugs

Tracey

When Rob Met Kari

Becoming a Shared Wife, Vol. 1 –

(Wife Sharing and Other Adventures)

Becoming a Shared Wife, Vol. 2 –

(Hazardous Wives)

Becoming a Shared Wife, Vol. 3 –

(Wives Who Stray)

Becoming a Shared Husband, Vol. 1 –

(Suck Me)

Becoming a Shared Husband, Vol. 2 –

(Husbands Who Stray)

Becoming a Shared Husband, Vol. 3 –

(Get even!)

Becoming a Shared Couple, Vol. 1 –

(Steamy Swingers)

Becoming a Shared Couple, Vol. 2 –

(The Share Thing)

Becoming a Shared Couple, Vol. 3 –

(Kathy is Wild)

Erotica Short Stories, Vol. 1 –

(Taboo Desires)

Erotica Short Stories, Vol. 2 –

(Nasty Steps)

Erotica Short Stories, Vol. 3 –

(Married But...)

Erotica Short Stories, Vol. 4 –

(Sizzling 10)

Erotica Short Stories, Vol. 5 –

(In My Wife's Panties)

Erotica Short Stories, Vol. 6 –

(Taboo Unlimited Desires)

Erotica Short Stories, Vol. 7 –

(XXX Stories)

Erotica Short Stories, Vol. 8 –

(Wild Urges)

Erotica Short Stories, Vol. 9 –

(Horny)

Erotica Short Stories, Vol. 10 –

(Stuffed Hard)

Erotica Short Stories, Vol. 11 –

(9 Shades of Sex)

Erotica Short Stories, Vol. 12 –

(Doing What She Does Best)

Erotica Short Stories, Vol. 13 –

(Hottest Nights)

A Weird One

Blackmailed MILF

Filthy Steps With My...

The Biggest She's Ever Had

Sharing Penny

Hardest Nights

My Woman's Dirty Secrets

She Makes Me...

She Needs More

My Wife's Inferno

Dirty Love

Hot & Tight

From the Author

WANT FREE COPIES OF MY BOOKS?
Just visit my blog and download free copies of my books:
awesomeauthors.org/justplainbob

Yes, I write about sluts and whores because as everyone knows, you tend to write about the things you know. And I do like sluts and whores, just not the ones that lie to me and cheat on me.

So be forewarned - if you click on a Just Plain Bob story you will be getting sluts, whores and husbands who do not kill, maim and destroy. There are other things you will rarely find in a Just Plain Bob story.

If you enjoyed any of my books then please share the love and promote my books in Amazon. I would really appreciate your honest reviews, too!

Good news is always welcome.

One Last Thing, For Kindle Readers...

When you turn the page, Kindle will give you the opportunity to rate this book and share your thoughts on Facebook and Twitter. If you enjoyed my writings, would you please take a few seconds to let your friends know about it? Because... when they enjoy they will be grateful to you and so will I.

Thank you!

Just Plain Bob
justplainbob@awesomeauthors.org

You may also like the books by these authors:

Less Than *Yesterday*

Lilith Jones

HOT ROMANCE EROTICA

"We said we wouldn't start a baby until we'd gone for a year without needing my paycheck," she said. It hadn't been a year, had it?

"Well, I wasn't talking about starting anything tonight. It's been more than eleven months. And, if we aren't going to make the goal next month, where is the huge expenditure going to come from? . . . Not to end a sentence with a preposition or anything."

"Ted! That's not really a rule."

"Yes, dear," Ted said, sounding like he thought she was trying to change the subject. He was probably right, too, but he didn't pursue the subject. Ted was, she kept reminding herself, nice.

Thursday, a few weeks later, she started a new disk of pills. That night, with Ted working late, she realized what that meant. If she did what they had agreed, it would be her last disk of pills for a good, long while. She thought for a minute about keeping them from meeting the conditions by dipping into her savings to buy a new, costly wardrobe. The account was in her name, after all; she needn't consult Ted. Really, though, she could delay the pregnancy more sensibly than that. She could tell him that she wanted to wait longer before they had a baby.

Then, though, she would have to tell him why. Even if she trashed her savings account, he would ask why. She did not want to answer. You could tell a guy you didn't love him anymore; you couldn't tell him that you still loved him -- but you loved him less. You certainly couldn't tell him that you were afraid to have a baby with him because you were afraid that you'd love him even less in five or ten years.

And she did want babies. She had been an only child of a single mother, and she wanted four. Ted, who had been the third of four, had warned her that she was romanticizing the experience. "Sure, I want kids. We'll have one, and we can decide about the next after we have some experience with that one."

That sure didn't leave her much wiggle room now. She wanted kids; she wanted Ted's kids. They might inherit his brains, and he would be a patient father. She wanted his kids, and she wanted to raise them with him. She just wasn't sure she wanted to be with him for another eighteen years to do the job.

But, if not Ted, who? She still loved Ted. Thinking that she might someday love him so little that she might want to leave him was no reason to leave him now.

Of course, single women had children every day. So leaving Ted wasn't deciding not to ever have kids. That was stupid, though. She was afraid of having a baby now because she was afraid of raising it as a single mother. She certainly didn't want to leave Ted -- merely feared that she would want to sometime in the future.

By the time that Ted got home, she was eager to see him, so eager that she was already in a sexy nightie.

"Have dinner?" she asked.

"Yeah. I brought you some left-overs if you want them for lunch tomorrow." She carried lunch; his cafeteria was so heavily subsidized that buying lunch at work was cheaper for him than brown-bagging it. Dinner after seven was free. Nothing was too good for programmers who stayed late. "Is it too late?" For sex, he meant.

"I adore Theodore." And, really, she still did. She hadn't used that silly couplet for a while, but it still applied.

"Well, I adore Jessica, too. Give me a few minutes, and I'll prove it." While he was in the bathroom, she took off the nightie. Then she got into bed and pulled the sheet up to her neck.

Ted got into bed without baring an inch of her. Then he leaned over and kissed her before resting on one elbow and slowly drawing the sheet off her.

"It must be Christmas. Santa brought me what I've always wanted." He kissed her again. Then his mouth trailed down to her right breast. His chin scratched, but the scratches were exciting. When his tongue and lips on her nipple had aroused her, she spread her legs. He stroked her cleft until she tensed.

"Ted."

"Yes." He moved over her and between her knees, which she raised. Then he opened her, filled her. "Jess." His chest hair tickled her nipples as he moved above her and inside her. She licked salt from where his neck joined his shoulder. Her arousal gyred upward with each of his strokes. The tension broke, and she thrust herself at him and around him.

"Jess," he said as she clutched around him. "Sssi," as he drove her into the mattress. "Cah!" as he throbbed within her contractions. He collapsed on her, and they gasped into each other's ears.

Somewhat later, he pulled himself off and lay on his side inches away. When she backed into him, he wrapped himself around her.

"You are," he whispered, "the sexiest woman in the whole world." They fell asleep in the spoon, although they woke on their own sides these days. She put the nightgown on and covered it with a bathrobe before cooking breakfast. They kissed lightly before going out the door on their separate ways to their separate work.

It wasn't that Ted ignored her satisfaction, she mused on the commute. He took care to bring her to climax every time. It was just that he brought her to climax in almost the same way almost every time. Ted was a considerate lover -- just as he was considerate about doing his share of the housework and letting her choose her share of their TV shows and her share of their entertainment and socializing. Ted was nice. Was nice enough?

If you enjoyed this sample then look for **Less Than Yesterday**.

Jack Ryder

L⚾VING My *Sitter*

Down and Dirty MILF
Hot Erotica

Aunt Marci wasn't really my aunt. At least, not biologically. She and my mother grew up in a foster home together and became very close. By the time they grew up and moved out on their own, they thought of each other as sisters. This continued even after mom got married and moved away with her new soldier husband. She always considered Marci her little sister.

Mom ended up being a single mother when my father was killed during a routine training mission. It was one of those fluke accidents that can happen when you've got a bunch of young men running around in a wooded area with guns and live ammunition. It was supposed to be a routine recon mission. But the men got spooked by reports that there were bears in the area. Dad was shot just at dusk by a young kid that mistook him for a bear.

I can't really say that being an only child of a single mother was difficult in any way. I never knew my dad and aunt Marci sort of filled that void during my early years. Despite being in her early teens, she was a wonderful nanny during those years. It provided mom the time to go back to school to complete her college courses. I always felt close to Marci even as a young boy.

By the time I reached my first year of college, mom had gotten her nursing degree and then her PHD in medical education. Marci had also earned her master's degree in nursing just before we moved away. I did not get to see Marci very often over the next two years. Mom accepted a professorship at a University in Oklahoma and Marci became a nurse at home in Ogden, Utah.

I won't bore you with everything that happened while I lived in Oklahoma, but there are a few significant things that I must pass on here. The first thing that happened was that I discovered that I could throw a baseball pretty well. I guess to be accurate I should tell you that I was soon considered a "Phenom" by the end of my first year of college. By the time the second year began, I already had pro offers and pro baseball scouts following me around.

As a result of my new found fame and notoriety, I also had a parade of young gorgeous girls that made it very obvious that they would drop their panties for me. This led to my second discovery. I loved the attention of women! But the weird thing was that I found most of the girls my age too shallow. I also found them too self-involved to ever measure up to the support and genuine nurturing that I had received from Marci and my Mother.

It was also during these two years that it finally occurred to me how absolutely sexy my nanny Marci was. I had not really ever thought about her in that way until she came to visit us that first Christmas after we moved away. Mom was working late those last couple of days before the Christmas break and I spent most of those evenings alone with Marci.

From the moment she came in the front door that first day of her two-week vacation, I could hardly take my eyes off of her. It was like my eyes were seeing her for the first time and what I saw was a tremendously sexy young woman. At five foot one, her 32D-22-33 figure made her an absolute little bombshell.

Her shoulder length auburn hair was long enough that if she let it fall forward, it could just cover her breasts. Like any true redhead, her skin is a soft milky white with little patterns of freckles on various locations. Her amber brown eyes look gold in the direct sunlight. Her full pouty lips make you wish you could kiss her endlessly.

I had an erection within minutes after she arrived that first evening. I did my best to conceal it as I carried her luggage into the house for her. I turned red as a beet when I saw her gaze between my legs as I dropped her luggage on the floor in the guest bedroom. I was relieved that she did not say anything about it as we went to the kitchen to make dinner.

I had an erection the entire time that I watched her cook our spaghetti dinner. Her perfectly round ass looked so damn sexy in the tight faded jeans that she had on. I found myself wishing I was twelve years older as I fantasized about pulling those jeans down and bending her over that counter top. I could almost swear that she found ways to wiggle her ass while she was going about her cooking. My dick would twitch each time she did it.

It appeared to me that a couple more buttons on her blouse were unfastened when she sat down at the table to eat. I could now see just the top of her frilly black bra. Because it was also a see through type material, I could clearly see the tops of her gorgeous milky breasts. It took every bit of my self-control to not stare at her tits while we ate.

I made small talk as we ate in an attempt to keep my mind off what it really wanted to focus on. I can honestly say that Marci was the very first girl I ever fantasized about. It started that evening as we ate dinner. My eyes secretly memorized every curve of her body, the small bumps in the center of her breasts, the way her pouty lips seemed to pulse as she ate her food.

"I heard that you are the star pitcher of your college baseball team." Marci's voice broke through a momentary vision of me fondling her tits. I felt a small ooze of fluid into my shorts as I lifted my eyes from her tits to her face. She was grinning slightly. "Yes...I do...Okay," I stammered as I felt a warmth radiating in my face.

"I guess that means you're good with your hands," she giggled playfully as she raised her fork to her mouth. I felt my dick twitch as she slowly placed the fork in her mouth then very sensually pulled it back out with her pouty lips pressed down on the tangs. "Yes...I guess....I am." I felt a shiver go up my spine as she slowly licked her lips then used her napkin to dab at the corners of her luscious mouth.

If you enjoyed this sample then look for Loving My Sitter.

JOAN VEGAS

Hot Dates
Being Sandwiched
MFM AND RELATED ADVENTURES

HOT ROMANCE EROTICA

According to leading Sociologists, the number of American women who have opened their lives to intimate affairs has substantially increased in recent years. It is estimated that as many as 60% of all married women have had affairs. That's right... 60%!

Yes, that's still less than the estimated 70% of all married men who are believed to have had affairs, but it reflects the fact that growing numbers of women are reaching out for sexual variety in their lives.

Sadly, traditional secret affairs still usually bring with them feelings of guilt and anxiety. Yet, it is understandable that women, just like men, want their sensual lives to be fuller, they want "newness," and they want the excitement of experiencing different partners and different sexual adventures.

I have always been a proponent of variety in sexuality for both men and women. But, I have advocated that couples share in the development of new pleasures for each other, that they intentionally allow each other to experience extra partner and that they actively participate in providing extra partners "as gifts" for their primary partner.

Some call what I advocate "open marriage." While I feel open marriages are far better than the traditional "closed," monogamous marriage, I feel that husbands and wives can enhance the open marriage concept by periodically inviting others to join THEM in bedroom play. I encourage couples to explore the addition of another guy or gal to their love play as a way to take an active role in providing their spouse with extra partners while doubling that spouse's sensual pleasures.

For decades (centuries?) men have talked to their wives about bringing an extra guy to their shared bed. Many men fantasize about watching their wife being serviced by one or more other guys. Sometimes it is the woman who proposes such a threesome (MFM - male/female/male, or female-centered threesomes). But, more often than not, the wife is the "hesitant" party, turned-on by the idea, but "hesitant" to really give it a try.

The following are comments gleaned from letters I have received over the last few years from women who have opened their lives to extra partners... not within the context of affairs, but within the context of threesomes or open marriage agreements. I will let them tell for themselves WHY they enjoy this way of expanding their feminine potential.

Joan

If you enjoyed this sample then look for **Hot Dates: Being Sandwiched**.

Ben E. Dorm

Mrs.
MOON
ROMANCE EROTICA

Conversation ceased when Mrs Moon entered. She paused and looked around, letting them see her as she gave the place the once over. It hadn't altered at all to her notice: ill-fitting, threadbare carpet, once blue but faded and dirtied by years of traffic, mostly scuffed and dirty work boots, all raggedy at the periphery and curled in one corner. The same old calendar hung on the wall, a bosomy young blonde smiling out, the young woman at least two years older than the year displayed in the calendar's header. A knackered settee sat against the back wall, while a remnant from some ancient kitchen stood in one corner, a freestanding unit brought in by someone to act as a surface upon which rested a kettle, a five litre bottle of water, and the makings for tea and coffee. There was a fridge next to the kitchen unit, unloved and unclean, its job being to keep milk cold during the working week as well as lager for the Friday afternoon drink-up. A low coffee table was in front of the sofa, much be-ringed by coffee and tea stains, an overflowing ashtray in its geograph-ical centre despite the no-smoking sign on display.

"Hello, Mrs Moon," one of the men said, a stocky, grey-haired man, his hair cut very short to his scalp. The man pushed himself upright from where he'd been leaning against the fridge, his arms folding across his chest as he moved. Mrs Moon knew him to be in his late forties, the foreman of the workshop.

"Tim," she replied, acknowledging the greeting. She surveyed the assembled group, eying each in turn. "Hello, boys," she breathed.

Three of the four remaining men mumbled their hellos, the trio wearing the same garb as Tim, grease-stained, baggy overalls. They were ubiquitous twenty-something's, one of whom Mrs Moon found rather attractive. The other two were nondescript, longish dark hair in need of a trim. In Mrs Moon's eyes they were unremarkable in every way, except to serve as extra meat in Mrs Moon's diet. She couldn't even recall their names – Alan and Pete or some such. Anyway, she had no interest at all in their personal lives or their circumstances. The young mechanics were always changing, with one leaving to be replaced by another, Tim being a constant in all the months Mrs Moon had enjoyed her Thursday afternoon sojourn in their company. She nodded at the trio, two of whom were sitting in the questionable embrace of the sofa, knees high because of insubstantial support in the sway-backed piece of furniture, the good-looking one sitting on the seat of an old ladder-backed chair, his arms dangling over the back support, the chair reversed beneath him.

The fifth man, the one standing with his back to the rear wall, the man in the suit, she ignored completely.

"Are you ready?" Mrs Moon asked, moving into the room with an exaggerated swing of her hips. "I hope so," she added, facing square on to the sofa, fists on her hips. "Because I'm so fucking horny…"

If you enjoyed this sample then look for Mrs. Moon.

DD WATSON

Punishing PUPPET

HOT EROTIC HARDCORE

Her head floated from side to side as she willed her eyes open. Her eyelashes parted to allow light in, but there was only darkness. The drug injected into her held her still even though her legs and arms were free.

She began to remember how she came to be where she was. The ride in the car trunk was by far bouncy but warm. When the trunk was open, her Master was there but didn't assist her out of it only his driver and another male she didn't recognize hauled her out. Before she could assess where she was the driver placed a patch on her neck, and her world went black again.

Puppet was never one to dwell on any negative situation. She trusted her Master Troy, no matter how mad he was with her breaking his rules he loved her unconditionally.

Going to the island was a set punishment but Puppet saw it as a learning experience. One she plans on succeeding in to make her Master proud.

She took in a deep breath and slowly exhaled it. That seem to help because she was able to move her fingers and toes sending a tingling sensation through her arms and legs. Puppet felt a growing chuckle inside her as if she was being tickled under her skin.

A smile spread on her cheeks as she tried to remain still to avoid another attack.

"You're awake," said the voice of a male that sat on the floor right beside her.

"Yes," she moaned. "You can see me?"

"Well yeah."

"So—it's not dark in here?"

"No it's very well lit you're just wearing a blindfold and the drug given to you is slowly wearing off."

"Oh, so where is the light coming from?"

"Window with a view of the garden showing a lovely sunny day."

"Why aren't you wearing a blindfold?"

"Because I'm here to watch you."

"Oh, so I'm on the island?"

"That is correct."

"Where's my Master Troy?"

"I'm not at liberty to say Puppet."

"And you know me. Am I allowed to be asking you questions?"

"With permission."

"By you?"

"No, by my Master—Shawn," he said, glancing up at the green eyed male who handpicked him out of a dozen. Took ownership, making him his personal pet; he stood clean shaven wearing black jeans, biker boots and shirtless. His long black mane hung loose on his shoulders. Two men stood behind him both wearing leather pants black boots and chest harnesses with buzz cut hairstyles.

"Is Master Shawn training me because I disappointed my Master?"

"He is."

"Is he listening to us?"

"Yes."

"Is he here in the room with us?"

He was signaled to silence by Shawn hovering his fingers in front of his pet's mouth. Shawn sat beside Puppet and leaned into her ear.

"I'm right here Puppet." His accent vibrated through her ears as she took in the heavenly scent that radiated from his skin.

Puppet enjoyed the tender time she was allowed to spend with him even though she hasn't laid eyes on him yet.

"That will be all Peter you may return to your duties."

"Thank you Master." On hand and knee Peter crawled out of the room followed by one of the males. Turning his attention back to Puppet, Shawn took his fingers and traveled over her naked skin, igniting the sensation that tortured her a moment ago.

Puppet tried to keep a straight face but regaining some movement in his limbs she began to squirm and giggle. Shawn only watched as she didn't try to push him away but seem to enjoy the torment. He watched her nipples harden as he flicked them with two fingers. Then running them between her legs he felt the wetness building in the soft folds of her crouch. He brought his drenched fingers to her mouth and pressed them pass her lips where she sucked and licked them clean. He removed them and rose to his feet.

"Get her to her knees on the floor and face her to the bed," he ordered a male who moved quickly to perform his task. Jerking Puppet up, he forced her into position as Shawn instructed.

Shawn walked over to a duffle bag opened in the corner and removed a handheld whip. The handle was as long as his arm with nine tails all knotted. When he returned his attention to Puppet, still blindfolded on her knees, he didn't hesitate. When the first strike landed she let out a deep cry that ricocheted around them. He landed another that resulted in the same. He picked up the tempo and continued to strike her back and arse until the welts glowed a profound red.

"How many blows did I give you Puppet?" He asked watching her claw at the mattress. "Answer me," he snapped striking her again.

"Six—teen—Master."

"Splendid, most pets never count. Troy has been training you."

"Yes Master—my Master is good to his pet."

"A little too good, or you wouldn't be here Puppet."

"Yes Master."

He switched the whip in his opposite hand and walked over to Puppet, snatching the blindfold from her eyes.

"Turn around Puppet and place your arms on the bed for support but remain on your knees."

"Yes Master." She turned clumsily but managed, getting her first glimpse of the notorious Shawn. The man whom her Master said strikes fear in any pet who crosses his path. Why was she not afraid? Was he just playing with her? She caught his emerald eyes, which shot ice daggers at her. His chiseled looks could rival her Master Troy's.

"Troy mentioned you were hard-headed. Who said you could look at my eyes?"

Puppet caught on, but it was too late as he began to whip her chest, stomach and thighs. The pain was more intense, but she kept her arm on the bed and didn't try to run away. Her Master Troy whipped her in this same manner on different occasions, so she grew to accept her punishments no matter how unforgiving they were.

When he stopped, she collapsed onto the floor at his feet breathing intensely but not unconscious.

"Take her to the groomers and tell them I'll call when I'm ready for her."

The male lifted Puppet up as if she didn't weigh a thing and draped her on his shoulder carrying her out of the room.

Peter had lied to Puppet, who was hanging upside down. She glanced around the room and saw no window only a ceiling light, mirrors and two doors.

Once Puppet was gone the second door opened, and Troy walked in wearing his full business attire. Shawn turned and smiled at his old friend from school whose dreams mimicked his.

"So what's your conclusion?" asked Troy.

"She's knows what she wants. I never saw a first timer take what she took from me. Or—maybe I've become soft."

"No, it's not you, Puppet is without doubt atypical. I can do anything to her, anything I wish."

"Then why bring her to me? Apparently you have a handle on her."

"No, she's become hesitant and explorative, not asking permission."

"She's evolving?"

"It has been five years. And as I said she'd taken my treatments without complaint."

"Do you want me to train her to be a dominatrix?"

Troy fell silent as he glanced to the floor. He closed his eyes and remembered his devoted pet and how she found him. Shawn's strong hand rested on his friend's shoulder waking him from his thoughts.

"It's been a long trip for you both, come and relax with me and let the groomer spoil her. A good meal, drink and sucking will clear your mind to make a decision."

That brought a grin to Troy's face as he let Shawn lead him out of the room.

If you enjoyed this sample then look for Punishing Puppet.